A Mother Dies at the Mishandling of Family Love

A Story of Family

ANGELI JOY LOWERY

authorHOUSE

AuthorHouse™
1663 Liberty Drive
Bloomington, IN 47403
www.authorhouse.com
Phone: 833-262-8899

Published by AuthorHouse 12/02/2020

ISBN: 978-1-6655-0989-3 (sc)
ISBN: 978-1-6655-0988-6 (e)

Library of Congress Control Number: 2020924083

Print information available on the last page.

Any people depicted in stock imagery provided by Getty Images are models, and such images are being used for illustrative purposes only. Certain stock imagery © Getty Images.

This book is printed on acid-free paper.

THE LOVE OF THE DAUGHTERS falls apart, before the mother dies, there is no love, that came out of it as of 3yrs 6mos now. From the oldest to the youngest only two of the daughters each separately communicate with one another the middle two daughters #2 Anita & #3 are close as possible & daughter #1 and daughter #4 are close to each other because of greed, which was sad the main thing the mother had wanted was for the (Four) 4 daughters was to all get along and love each other … .which is further from the truth. Happening. The oldest daughter is born in 1960, 2nd daughter born in 1962, 3rd daughter born in 1964 and 4th daughter was born in 1968. The oldest daughter name is Twana, second born is Anita third daughter is Tonya & fourth daughter is Anna Marie. The 1st daughter and the second daughter are the only to that had kids and their union of kids are not even communicating with each other because of what the 1st daughter and the 4th daughter did to the 2nd & 3rd daughter. They didn't know how to grieve the life & death situation of our mother's illnesses. The four ladies/sisters mother went through a lot of difficult times while having an ill mother & transferring her from (1) one daughter to the other for care for years until tragedy struck our family our mom was placed in a hospital because of family neglect ambulance had to come to the younger daughters house to get our mother out before there was a death on the fourth daughters hands Thanks to God first the husband and this wife (myself) we made a decison to secure the fate of our mother's ♥ life ... with God's help first & our mother getting impossible strength, she was alive to go to Alleghany General Hospital 320 E North Ave, Pittsburg, PA 15212. Having a difficult decision to make a decision because of the mothers oxygen low levels being cut off or lowered every day our mother slipped into a coma doctor gave the 2nd daughter Anita less than 24 hours to make a decision to cut her throat so they could save her life and take her off of oxygen forever. It was the hardest decision the daughter had to make (ever). With love, emotions, tears, fears, hurts, lack of trust coming from all directions she felt so alone in her decision making. So with the help of my stepdaughter I decided to say yes by cried & prayed first because the doctor at Alleghany General Hospital said it had to be done. Because of the oxygen had been cut down by daughter #4 because she wanted our mom out of her house for always accusing her of stealing her mother's money. Not because it was true or not, but she was accused on a regular bases. Because our mother was going through a beginning stages of Alzheimer's disease, and our mother needed her love, endurance, understanding, respect, patience, prayers godly wishes, but because our mother was going through early stages of dementia a mental illness that causes someone to be unable to think clearly or to understand what is not real. The Alzheimer's disease it is a usual process condition that is marked by deteriorated cognitive functioning often with emotional pathy it's the bording on dementia. But because of the stress that Anna Marie was going through on their job and all the evil spirits that was dealing with her she wouldn't take our mother the doctor's no more to her appts or take her to pickup her medicines anymore. Other family members had to go to CVS and Rite Aide to retrieve her meds, and take her to her doctors appts. The 3rd daughter Tonya and the 2nd daughter Anita and her granddaughter Dominique all had to resume responsibilities for our mother and our Aunt Jeanine had to do all things for her as well. Anita 2nd daughter had a job and Tonya 3rd daughter had a job out of town and Dominique the granddaughter had .(2) jobs so they all had to work, and work it out in shifts, which was difficult at times. All because of mishandling and misunderstanding between the 4th daughter & their mother because she was dating again all of the daughters has been married several times. The youngest sibling because she was dating again all of the daughter was going through her own personal stresses. The mother and daughter #2 & granddaughter of number #2's daughter Dominique had to be given gas money because they lived in different cities and county in Pennsylvania but two of them out of four daughter's had the most patience with the mother at this time because of her illness and grandmother being her issue was oxygen she had to be transported with a machine of oxygen in her nose and in a wheel chair up and downstairs because the mother was bought back and forth on both levels of the fourth daughter Anna Marie house because she didn't want her mother right in front of the door but it was easier for their mother if she was because the kitchen was on first level of the house the bathroom was also on the 1st level of the house but the mother had to crawl up & down the steps to bathe herself while the fourth daughter worked.

Our mom Ellen Trone had to be in the front of the door because she was ill but she was helping out her family taken care of her 2nd great granddaughter her granddaughters daughter because she was in a crisis in the family the granddaughter not the grandson and great grandmother was the only family member left who was entrusted to keep them because of the family tragedy Nicole great granddaughter had endured, when she was 6yrs. old twice. So the trust of other family members wasn't happening & the kids of the two elders daughter's #1 Twana Trone and #2 Anita Trone never put their kids in daycare of preschool the care of all their children was always entrusted to their grandmother. 5 grandkids split between sibling #1 & sibling #2. The children was kepted in the many mansion big house in Pittsburgh PA on the Eastside which got burned down & got sold which all four adult/ladies agree on this, but couldn't agree on anything else so orphan's court in Alleghany County had to take over. So I advice anyone who has property that has to be divided by being left to your children and they don't really get along that good have a will in place or orphan's court records/will orphans court division will handle it for your family and a representative of the courts appointed attorney will receive most of the family's money because of the negligence of the family aunt was negligent because of my grandmother.

The family having to have the mansion sold a legacy house built for 100 yrs. of age nice sturdy home, which our mother Ellen Trone tried to keep up with taxes on the house and paying people to do the work family friend, bringing in her daughter and her daughters kids to do inside cleaning and the 4th daughter

Anna Marie to do yard work Anita Trone—Bluebird for them all it was alot of work which it sold for $80,000 the money was suppose to be divided amongst for sibling be other DNA greedy family member came along for the ride didn't receive much because nothing from nothing leave nothing so if you put nothing into something you end up with nothing. So the court appointed attorney stepped in which turned out to be great he prevailed and the property money got split more corrected then not. The youngest sibling cheated the other 2 siblings me and my sister Tonya out of burier arrangements right by her lies and cheating but the courts found out about the truth before it was too late and that's the power of God she ended up with the less money beside she got the money for insurance only because it came to her house and she show the insurance company the false document of a proxy she was awarded $20,000 for her mothers death. Our mother death which should have also been divided four ways. The 1st sibling Twana Trone-Burros and Anna Marie Trone made the review of body arrangement & got her clothes together & picked out her casket and other stuff that come with funerals. As important to have your will in place so greed family member siblings won't cheat other siblings and family member out of what they all deserve. The family was divided separated, our families God teaches us all to not lean on your own understanding but to trust in the Lord by putting God 1st he works for your good, Our mother left money $30,000.00 in cash behind, at the hospital, it was stolen from my daughter the 1st daughter took the money from the hospital, and brought it to her oldest daughter whom brought it to the bank at the bank of North West savings bank in Smithfield St Pittsburgh PA …

she was in town to bring the money to the bank … .

The niece Dominique Bourboura the 1ˢᵗ sibling Twana and the 4ᵗʰ sibling

Anna Marie had false papers proxy drawn up and a false notary as well, before

that the police had to be called because the 4ᵗʰ sibling Anna Marie had blocked

Dominique and her husband Drew Bourboura in there driveway and they

couldn't go to work so the mother called she told her what the 4ᵗʰ sibling Anna

Marie was doing so Anita Trone—informated them she was a lawyer not the

police and she couldn't make a citizen's arrest and got the police involve they

made her get out of there drive way so they could go on with their life. That's

when the other two sibling #1 and #4 come up with the false document to go to

the bank by #4 tried to cheat them all out of the money and ended up with the

less of all which was great. Whose laughing now. Thank God all dealings with

each other is over we don't have to see or hear from each other again which is bad

a farther the truth because all our mother ever wanted was for all her daughters

she gave birth to just love each other and get along.

It was sad how the four adult/ladies couldn't agree on anything not even to

the will to one another it end up two against two. But God will make a way out

of the no way that all four of these female myself is included in this will never be

close or our generation won't be in touch with each other social media was the

only other way of making contact & the oldest sibling is even deleted blocked

from that as well. Anita car had been reposed so she gave the mother Ellen Trone

car she gave her to the estate to be sold but being she ended up with money from her deceased mother my mother I have a brand new car because my husband Rodney Bluebird had to work I had to work and had no means of transportation but now I do, but I am disable because of accidents with a bad back, osteoporosis God has chosen to sit me down because I was such an active female always walking long walks plenty miles on the tracks of colleges taken my family to parks for long walks it was time to settle down and do life differently. My life is now drama free and I owe it all to God who made it all possible, back to our life while our mother was in the hospital being neglected I was always visiting her in her car while I had it before I turned it over to her estate I was always visiting our mother she informed me by writing she wasn't get bathe on a regular bases, so I was out shopping for good pencil for her to write and note pad for her to inform me of how her days was Ellen Trone my mother love to write that where I got my writing from the handwriting looks like hers but she had secretary skills. I use to but it has been along time since I wrote in grade school but she didn't get bathe for two days at a time she loved to take showers every day, I do as well so when I informed them she wasn't getting bathe they did nothing about it. So when she told me I hurt for our mother. They would sedate her so she would be sleep when I came. But my mom was smart she would leave me a note and write what she wanted done. Or things she needed the hardest job I ever had was to watch my mom remain in the hospital until she went home to God.

The hospital was moving her from upstairs to downstairs to closed in a glass room she was afraid of daughter she stated to me 2nd daughter and 2nd granddaughter that sibling #4 tried to kill her. That she was going to do it slowly by turning off her oxygen do so low everyday so she couldn't get enough air to breath sibling #4 would come home from work and take her wheelchair upstairs to the 3rd level of her house and neglect and ignore her own mother our mother Ellen Trone after turning down her oxygen low this is so sad to do to your own mother who didn't want anymore kids after the 3rd sibling of ours because she knew she would have to struggle raising 4 children/adults without a husband's full support. But she gave birth to this fourth daughter so instead of feeling grateful your alive to have a life you try and kill your own mother. You call your sister who had a husband that wasn't totally stabled in a rented house but you had been paying a mortgage on your house for years and they now had step kids living in our house single family home vs your townhouse and cause us more drama but thank God the husband Rodney Bluebird and me Anita Trone-Bluebird smart enough not to allow that to happen chicks on drugs tried to live in our home. Me said no. The man growed up with girlfriend. Who grew up with step cousin to Tony Braxton Joann Battlefield Debbie Braxton sister Debbie Braxton & Ellen Braxton sister her boyfriend of Joann Battlefield her boyfriend and his first baby mother did 10yrs in prison, got out of prison and she became his girlfriend Joann Battlefield her boyfriend Kevin Brown choked her up, a couple of times in front of me and my husband because of her smart mouth, but that's no excuse to abuse your woman they broke up because she was cheating on him with other guys and he takes on another girlfriend, Kevin Brown my husband very good friend and she cheats on him to alter off few parties that they come to at my house he goes back to old girlfriend sleeps with her she's takes a picture of him shows it to his girlfriend by text message & picture, she goes out cheats on him as well he comes home in an hated argument because she slept with her ex-boyfriend & got money for it. They have a heated argument and he chokes and kills her too. Leaves the scene goes to his sister's house where he is caught by the FBI, goes back to prison for life and to finish the life term he had @ 7 years added on. I thought he was a very nice guy I like Kevin Brown I really did like him and these are some of the people that wanted to live in my house. Our rented house because it was a single family thank God for the good sense of my husband and me Anita for not allowing that to happen. I went out to vote in the new voting location in a church well, when I got to the church it immediately jump out to me in my heart so I told my husband because he went with me to vote I want us to become full members of this church, because my husband couldn't vote @ the time but he agreed, so we him and we started going to our church and our lives began change we my husband and me was look for a church home for years. In 2011 we found this church we both love enjoy this church United Baptist Church.

In 2011 we both became full member's of this church of liberty Mt Ararat Baptist Church 116 South Highland Ave Pittsburgh Allegheny County PA. My husband Rodney Bluebird became the usher of our church while I became the door greeter and love the position of our church I go to bible study at 10:00 am leave class @ 10:45 am go to the door greet everyone who comes in with a smile some I know with a smile & hugs & compliments and all who come through the door, a welcome to all new, never seen, before people talk with those who ask question we have all kind of people who come to our church after 11:15 am I come in the church sanctuary and join my family and get to respect and enjoy the service with the folks fellowshipping I go home from service at 12:45 pm pickup my daughter from work. Eat relax play with my games on my cell phone cook dinner prepare myself for the next day by 5:00 pm I leave go back to church when I enjoy our urban service where I get to enjoy informal service on Wednesday I go to bible study where God is really moving me in my life toward greatness I don't curse anymore and when I am provoked to anger which everyone is I immediately ask God for forgiveness and tell him here we go again I am not perfect or a perfect person in Christ in my spiritual walk but I am walking following Christ through the will of God according to his will and trying to stay on his path.

We are separated because of friends and family in our personal business. I am living with my daughter taken care of her two year old son, while she works and my husband is living with his daughter doing the same thing except he works but we come together, we are best friends we share intimacy because we are working on straighten our lives out before we decide to totally move on. I personally don't believe in divorce we got divorced out from our spouses before each other came back into each other's life which to me is crazy the daughter now has a man of her own thank God and the mother too, his ex-wife. Our love was strong that was built on a friendship that has a strong bond as friends only. Which is not my husband, a man her own age. And I have two deceased husbands before him. I'm in love with Christ and I am happy because I don't have nobody kids/ adults trying to move in my house trying to take over it. … while they have street ladies running in and out used to come over once a week before separation begin while they have a layed back father tolerating. I will have no one in my home leaving lights on all night TV going all night making bills you can't pay. Not going through alot of fussing and arguing, no body nobody in my home drinking beers smoking cigarettes leaving trash around the house. No one controlling my TV's my husband got the remote control of my TV's in my bedroom when he comes over to visit I cook and clean up behind him but it's not often that he comes over like only once a week maybe we entertain each other I cook him a meal with a drink a dish and wash his clothes get him to stripe down to his under wear because I don't like germs on my bed. I forgot to say I am a germaphobic person asthmatic as well sorry I forgot that part.

Sorry I forgot that part. Very sensitive and allergic to everything that's one of the things my husband didn't like about me, to sensitive but it's my life. He has issues to skin is too close to his vein if you touch them the wrong way he flips out. I don't like that about him. Man has to have the last word I don't like that either, and he wants people to love him for him and don't try to change him, his character but he wants to be king but not allow me to be queen and be (me). I have to be the queen he wants me to be and be totally controlled by him. I don't mind listening to him because God says to be submissive to your husband but I feel you have to be equally yoked in order to make this stand in some areas we are in some area's we are not my husband was pushed by his mother to do stuff and if a repair person came to the house to do work for the mothers house so she would not have to keep paying the repair guy. My husband would be forced to sit and talk with the repair guy so he would learn exactly what they did and he could do the repair next time to save money for the family. The way I see things for a male child grow up with a mother working all of week and two other siblings not much older than you by a year or two having to learn everything quickly before your time had to be hard on the child, but he did it and he is advance beyond his years my husband got out in the streets and he knew stuff my mother knew who was in her 70's when she died they had conversations my husband and my mother, but I was sheltered, so I had no idea what they was talking about half the time, I would listen just to try and learn but half the times I did not understand what they was talking about my husband Rodney Bluebird and my mom Ellen Trone, she and he they could talk for hours. And they did. My mother was well educated she went to the Community College of Alleghany County she was a nurse's aide candy striper at the hospital she worked at the government's printing office she cooked (cashiered she worked for Grayhound Bus terminal where she received the money to get on buses for travel from state to state, she worked at a bar downtown then she worked at a store that kept getting robbed at gun point it was alot on her she became afraid to live in the city where her daughter #4th lived, she wanted to move back to the county of Alleghany Pittsburgh PA badly she worked her last job before she retired for the county for 15 yrs. From family dollar to dollar tree 123 North Sheridan Ave East Liberty PA 15206—3018 she transferred from 700 E. Warrington Ave, Pittsburg, PA 15210-1562 our mother endured lots of changes in her lifetime and her Christian walk she was about to attend a church. So she never fell to watch it on television & hear the service by via radio she loved reading the bible for a while I didn't get it she use to tell me to stop cursing but I went through alot of changes in my life as well.

I was bulled by my own sister Twana growing up because of her jealousy for me. I had longer hair was always told I was the pretty one when it only was two girls before the other two came along. The older sister the jealous one used the little ones to make me jealous by always saying they were her kids and none of them was mines. But when my mom was home which wasn't often she would say one was mines and one was her's. She would tell my little sister's to do evil stuff to me, so they wouldn't like me. My elder sister was demonic she had 3 kids by 3 different men. Twana was fast and competitive very much I was shy, so she took advantage of me, but from her evil spirit, I learned how to curse and kick, my mother who worked 3 jobs to take care of her kids four girls, was always getting reports from the elder sibling, but the mother was tired from working so hard to whoop us was impossible. My elder sibling never told what the other two little sisters did she always lied on me to see me getting whippings she would bite kids and say I did it. She would kick, slap, beat kids up, and say I did it. And she was smart because she always covered her tracks by saying, if you tell, I will get you again. So the kids would be scared to own up to the fact the truth to their own parents about the truth of who really did the dirty deed to them. One day I had a little girlfriend she really liked me, and I liked her. But my evil sister beat her up and told her if you tell I will get you again just like she told the rest of the kids she would beat up. She was mad at the girl because she liked me, and I like her I was upset that she beat her up and bit her up all over her body. I cried while she was doing these thing to my friend, the girls parents went to give her a bath and saw the bite marks. She told her parents I did it. Because my sister instructed her to say this. Twana told her that the story better not change, and so when her parents and her came to deal with me and my parent even though I didn't do it. My mother whooped me really bad in front of the girl and her parents she was crying watching me get a beatings for something I didn't do & her parents asked her why are you crying for her? She wouldn't say until she got home, because my evil sister was watching also and laughing at me, but as soon as Michelle got home she told her parents the truth she said Anita didn't do it, that why I am crying, because her big sister did it. And she told if I tell the truth she would get me again. So I couldn't watch Anita get such a bad whooping because she was my friend and she cried why her sister beat me up and bit me up, all over my body which was very mean and evil, out came the truth and her parents and her came back to my house and told my mother the truth that my sister did it, which was very mean and evil.

That is why it is important for family/families to have a will because when you have evil jealous siblings and evil kids who steal from their own mother you have to protect your children/adults future. It's very important to have a (will) you will have greed and greedy children, mean, demonic spirited adults who will fight, lie, make up stuff. Just like you see lies in soup opera's and empire these cut throat back stabbing sibling exist, and lies in housewives, you will see lies in families the same way. Who will fight you through court or the jail system or the street system or by any means possible dirty underhanded females, males, whoever are around to take what you have because of jealousy or any greed hatred reason who don't care about you or the quality of life who don't know Jesus or the value of life whose been end and out of jail for different fraudulent reasons and will do hurtful things to destroy your life because she don't value life at all and is out for money only not because they should love their families just the saddest thing ever. I grew up feeling like an orphan child now I have a good Christian family everybody is in church, they are holy thank God for my new family they love me just like I love them.

I was only 19 yrs old so you can image how devastating it was for me. My 1st finance was a great provider who wanted to take me out of the state buy a home together to live with him and his family I loved his family and they love me his mother and my mother had the same birthday but we were 13 yrs apart he was the oldest I wasn't mature enough for that relationship he taught me how to drive loved my kid took very good care of them until I left him because I felt controlled I wish I did things differently but I am being total honest here with my life. And my 3rd husband another very good man who I will always respect and love mainly because he never cheated on my sexually. Yes he went out with other women but he was exploring their minds not there bodies and I trust him explicitly in 9 ½ year or I never slept with another person sexually because we were together married in ever since of the word we had alot of outside interference in our marriage but honestly the love was always there sexually.

My new family loves me unconditionally my mom she is the greatest mamie my sister Deshell same age as my 1ˢᵗ DNA sister Twana and she loves me tell me all thing Christian I should know to better my life for me all kind of good advice I have a Uncle James he is understanding and respectful to me as well I have a brother Stevey who is kind and a niece Rionna she is beautiful smart in college young precious my new family is great thanks be to God my daddy is deceased also he died 8 yrs before my mom he was older than my mom same age as my grandmother I guess my mother like them older too, I also liked them older in the beginning my 3ʳᵈ husband Rodney Bluebird was younger not by much 1 yr and 11 mos. exactly. 2 husband's older and a finance older, the rest of my male friends younger. But my last husband was wise beyond his years. So it's like he's older also. I seem the youngest at times my husband's very intelligent know's alot about life even though he didn't get it all right growing up his self he is wiser than the average man his age he has old man sense wisdom I am like a baby when it comes to what he already knows street wise I have alot of book smart and experience not worldly like him. But I am smart too. I am left hand which also means I think with both sides of my brain I have a sibling who is left handed as well that's why I know.

She is very smart two. Anna she's the only child that my parent had that went to preschool because my parents couldn't afford it but her father put her in preschool I know that's why she thought she was smarter than the rest of the four sibling but she is now grown up she went after my boyfriends never got even one of them. One of my male friend. I don't know if she was just being evil or seriously trying to get them but it never worked. We are 6 years apart. My first husband slept with one of my cousin is a horrible enough thought in your head while your pregnant so I've always had handsome men in my life finances husband's, boyfriend my so called friends and cousin always came after my male friends, which is pretty sad. Because that mean they never was woman enough to find a man of there own. LOL, which was no consolation for me. None of the men I can remember was faithful accept my first fiancée 2nd fiancée 3rd husband that all. 1st finance was of 20 yrs, 2nd one was immature and not ready for our serious relationship but was ready to put me in a home. No thank you. My 2nd boyfriend died by the hands of his dad killed him Louie Pole, his sister Shavinie & Deon & 2 cousin are the only survivor the daddy was a janitor who lost his job and mind at the same time (Luke 10:19, Behold, i have given you authority to trend on serpents & scorpions and over all power of the enemy and nothing shall hurt you rejoice in your names are written in heaven)

Interested in sleeping with no one else. I can say that for him because I can't and I won't speak for anyone accept myself. I kept my husband's satisfied 3rd husband and I were one in the bedroom it was the jealousy of a family that totally damage the marriage but he knows as well as I do. Misery has always love company and in some families I personally don't think it will ever change, it don't matter because for almost 10 yrs straight I shared with him spent time with him the will never ever have and we both loved it, to God be the glory enough about people who have never care for me I am a better woman because of it, I have really grown and recognized how much I have arrived. I will name a few people who didn't really want us together his 2nd ex-wife 3rd son 4th of the people in the streets who told him that they had me, but the only wish they had it so good. I loved him so much back to my family, my thoughts, & opinions other families should have a (will) written up and power of attorney in place & if you change your (will) due to neglect change it with a notary right away so when tragedy strictens and it will.

A family you cannot fight one another over what is written & rightfully yours. What is legally bound and what is yours and so extended family won't come up just because the share the same name as you and think they deserve something when we all know you did nothing to help my mother with her property when her home burnt you were nowhere around to help clean-up paint gutter out by everybody & they grandmother had their hand out the like or even deserved something none of them didn't and that why they all accept one got a sizable check due to the death of his father which was my cousin son who was also deceased at the time. So if your family members know you are close to the end get your life in order get your life right with Christ first paper work second your insurance third and your funeral arrangements fourth decide your proxy because you can be cheated out of this as well. We almost was by God step in hand handled it the rest of the way because family can be dirty for real. So if you feel you're not being treated right get your will notarized ASAP because the kind of fight for what was once yours is horrible in families

Twana oldest

Anita 2nd oldest

3rd was Tonya

4th was Anna Marie

No love, no God, no respect, no honor amongst thieves four girls 2 against 2. Meaning 2nd & 3rd are speaking associating and loving each other through life challenges and 1st and 4th are speaking tolerating each other. 2nd and 3rd get alone, 1st & 4th even @ the review of the families the police had to be called in the nonsense of the 1st and 4th sibling trying her darnest to set up the 2nd and 3rd the 3rd knew they had evil games but the 2nd which was myself wasn't nothing going to keep me from reviewing my mother's body before the funeral and every dirty trick in the book was tried by the 1st and 4th sibling Twana & Anna Marie, Anna Marie lied to the courts to get trumpeted up charges pressed on her sibling 3rd sibling our sibling Tonya because they wanted the 2nd sibling me Anita and 3rd sibling Tonya to miss the review of our mother's body plus the funeral to make the 1st sibling Twana and 4th sibling Anna Maria look good by having us locked up on false charges so the rest of the family wouldn't know what they really are like and what devious things that the both of them are capable of Anna Marie told the judge that Tonya poured aides blood on her which was a dirty lie, as well as the guns in the trunk of my our mothers car she gave me because they wanted me shot died or behind bar but serving an ontime God wouldn't, allow any of their devious wickness prevail. Third sibling Tonya was a CPA not a nurse or doctors that lie was not possible the judge through it out. Tonya didn't show up to her mothers own review, but she came ready to the funeral with a sheriff to serve the 4th sibling @ our mothers funeral which was great because she was living in the city and we lived in the county and that was the only way she could be served. And she didn't show up because she didn't want to be around her fake sibling to the present on the 4th sibling, because she wanted to get her served in court of the things she was doing to us, and for a hearing to stop all the drama, because of what she did to us. Before the review of the body and after because she also went to the 5th district lied on me before our mother was even decease Ellen Trone our mother I never stole a car ever to scared of a female never touched a gun ever but she was so smart but I was not smart enough to know this. I was protecting our mother Ellen Trone from her and from her putting her in the streets, when she was to move in with me she informed our mother Ellen Trone that I was about to be homeless which was further than the truth she wanted her to move in with the older sibling Twana. But our mother had asked me to get her car and her clothing her purse most of her stuff and she also helped me put her things in our mother Ellen Trone car to drive off it. They turned around and told the police I stole her car crudy. All my life I was afraid of guns and my own husband owned a gun and I have never touched it. I was a virgin to weapons never played with toy guns not even cop's and robbers. Barbie dolls yes guns no. Never. I heard my mom say she got robbed on the job a couple of times I got robbed by a knife. Not guns. Gun in stupid people hands kills, told me that they could have shot me dead the cop's when they pulled me over for weapons in the trunk which I never had any weapon's ever, and police asked me why would my DNA tell such a dirty lie on me like this. She hated me. And I had a letter with my ill mothers name on it saying I never stole her car plus I had insurance cards with her and my name on them, and the insurance in our name my mother and myself. The police say being our mother Ellen Trone is in hospice illed like this your 4 siblings should be coming together in love not being devious evil mean & vindictive like this try to destroy your sibling life pitiful. They let me go to work the apologized said they were trying to do their job. I thanked them for not killing me and broke down & cried got it back together and went to work. I was a school teacher take care of preschool children, from that day forth been skeptical about them females ever since one went to jail for welfare fraud. And the other thought she was a cop. (renta cop). And my sibling had cancer not AIDS so I just want to clear that up. I want to clear this out because a serious lie was told as God is my witness it's not true it was a false statement to hurt not only my sister but it was talking about it hurt the closeness we could have had because of Twana's lies on Tonya never had AIDS, she had cancer. And the statement against her wasn't fair to our family because of the jealousy and lies by the two sisters Twana and Anna Marie, the first and the fourth sibling.

Our mother Ellen Trone, was a loving mother God is great and always will be our mom was getting moved from the city hospital to county (hospice) for recovery and to heal her throat which she was off oxygen now, the other two siblings Twana and Anna Marie lied and said they were her proxy which that document was forged they showed the fake document to the hospital the two of them put together. The older sibling Twana was a cop and the youngest was in law school. I was a teacher 2nd sibling and the 3rd sibling was an accounting with a four year degree from Morgan State University in Baltimore MD. All four sibling was very smart ladies but the matriarch of the family who held the family together until she got ill and they lost everything, dignity, respect, love, understanding endless possibilities, intelligence, loyalty, faithfulness, responsibility, independence, character, wisdom, godliness, sisterhood, family, everything that our mother had instill in us was gone for one another. Because of the sister rivery hurtful crudy things was happening the oldest got divorce 2nd oldest got separated 3rd sibling and her husband is still together 4th sibling was already divorced from her husband before any of this happened because her husband was cheating on her on the internet and he cheated on her and she killed his baby because when she went to the doctors for appt she had a disease so she killed the baby through abortion. Sorry about your husband but the world didn't do it she did. She is not seeing her husband since they got separated. They talk of course in the process of divorce.

She caught him cheating on the internet. Our mother Ellen Trone, was put in hospice care after two months she died in front of my eyes heart attack's end kept she was alive until her last daughter arrive and she was gone. She stayed in hospice care she was transfer from floor to floor she wasn't bathe regularly like she liked or I like based on all messages she left me, she was sedated when I come to informed me where to look for her note and I found them. When she was a wake she was always nervous I knew because her leg shakes like minds but her's was jumping shaking when she didn't get her nerve pills jumping on its own. Ellen Trone our mother could write but not talk. Because the hospital cut her throat because the lowered oxygen damaged her lungs even worst because of neglect in the home where she lived it really messed her up, she was smart and had a good memory she remember lots of stuff we would discuss funny thing we celebrated both of them. When I came to visit her every day, and do her feet massages. This day right here is thanksgiving day which affects me in two ways 1 (our) my mother is no longer with us. 2 This is the day before (our) my grandmother's birthday 27th or 28th but both of them but for what I have learned was on harvest day (halloween) was, with my husband Rodney Bluebird and the grandkids my pastor said a quote from the bible which stuck with me Absence from the body means present with the Lord and the funny thing is my husband had been saying this for years. But it meant nothing to me because I was in grieving process but harvest day it was over 3yrs and 6 mos. but I was so buried in my grief for my mother I couldn't hear him, and I didn't understand until my pastor said it. And after he said it because I had been crying this day all my tears just went away all the worries it all left me that night. It was finally rescued from it the same night. God opened up my heart, my mind & my spirit and I received the total message, I finally had a dream on November the 10th about my deceased mother my husband Rodney Bluebird had an accident that day car totalled. That night she & I was in the alley in an old neighborhood she had to go to work it was dark we both was nervous to go through the alley so she got her clothes on we ran through the alley at the end of the alley my husband was waiting for us, and as of today.

As of today I can't make sense of that dream. One of my friends taught me how to look it up, but I've been busy with my life, my husband Rodney, my grandkids, my own illness. 🙏 Now i have Respiratory issues I now have to thank my daughters husband who left me with this virus the was very ill & coughed all over the place not covering his mouth his germ I am a germopho, I asked him what he was taken to stop him from spreading his germs & I got expose by him not coving up his germs. Told him to gargle to help his to stop passing germs now I am ill. Back and forth to urgent care Kaiser trying to get better so I can finish my book and close this chapter in my life, my thumb is inflamed with arthritis and triggered thumb this is the second surgery because of my accident she had my thumb done it was a successful surgery, but I have great friend one of them have turned me on to rubbing sports alcohol it's for muscles aches stiff joints and it works very well I thank God for great friends.

Back to her stay in the hospital they left an IV in my mother arm her left arm from the city hospital so when we were in the county hospital she was trying to tell me about the IV and I didn't understand she was putting the IV out because the always had her strapped down with her arms I felt bad because my mother was always free spirited but they thought she was going to put the thing at her throat so they would tie her hand it looked so bad like she was a prisoner. I hurt for her and all she kept telling me was don't leave me here to die I would cry when I got alone because I felt guilty of leaving my mother there when I had no control over her life and my sister claimed she was trying to get my mother moved from the county hospital to a better hospital when she knew that it was a lie she wasn't trying to do anything because she was happy mother our mother was there because of the lies the 1st sibling & the 4th sibling had take and showed the fake proxy the two of them had control of my mother life at first the doctors was not trying to help me make sure my mother was getting everything she needed they was not making sure she got bathe changed and was comfortable they put her in a glass room

Glass room like she was poison. They thought she had leprosy and she didn't. My siblings would come to the hospital tell my mom lies that I was losing my house that at the time was not true. We was fine, accept my stepdaughter had moving with us with her baby mother baby daddy drama she had a son going on 3 yrs of age not potty training she was running away from her baby daddy in New Jersey to West Virginia to Pittsburg PA to live with her mother who only bought her up here to brake up me and my husband because and she was evil and go chased away from where they lived at gun point my husband ex-wife daughter & her son there son just got out of jail and wanted to come here to ruin our marriage and didn't want to see or hear that me and my husband was happy and that after a year of divorcing them he had moved on with his life our life of 10yrs now they been divorce and 11yrs. In Jan that he divorced her. But never loved her I was his second love of his life and the loyalty the faithness is still there even though we are separate because of his family moving her and interfering with our marriage having her from them all. But God is a jealous God but also an awesome God and reigns in heaven and on earth put. God first in all you do. It works for our good. I plead the blood of Jesus over my book and the success of it all. Keep evil demonic spirit away and look out for my family. The will of God having a plan please everybody, listen for your own good. Thanks be to God for allowing me the mind, the strength, the spirit, the body, and the soul to be able to put all this together in Jesus' name it works for our good and I dedicate this book to my mother, Ellen Trone, thanks be to God for putting all this together.

The stepdaughter and I become close I potty trained her 3yrs old son talked her into quitting alcohol and she going back to college get her credits for her degree she is now a pharmacy technician with a job had a baby in our house boyfriend lived there too. The made bills high in our house she moved out back into the mother house from getting put out of her apartment and the mother put her back in the streets this time with two kids my husband and I talked her into going into the shelter were my son has to live with his baby mother & all of her hundred kids (kidding) 6 kids and so I knew how the shelter work he help my step daughter Jacquil get back on her feet through the shelter now she has a place a church have a life of her own temporary has my husband stay with her while I am temporary stay man my daughter my step son has a car now thank you Jesus my husband ex-wife has a boyfriend now thank you Jesus we come together for the grandkids birthday partys she still nasty with her smart mouth but I know Jesus and I know a LPN Practice license nurse ain't got nothing on me and my husband he's never loved her but always loved me so nothing for me to be ever be jealous.

But God is an awesome God throughout all my endeavor how my pain my mom watched we walk across the stage twice I did not even know I was coming across the stage the second time but I had high honors 3.88 GPA in Medical Billing and Coding my husband sacrifice his education so I could graduate we were in a program together he started before I did he was going to graduate as a

Medical Assistant but decided to allow me to finish my higher learning instead his grades were low even though he's smarter than I am my school grades looked better than his so he withdrew because it was costing us a lot I worked for the school in the administration office part time and went to school full time had a car accident and has to stop school for a month or two went back for school had to wait out because my schedule class wasn't ready or available and I went back to school a month later and was able to go back and graduate after 18 mos. of school but it was hard to find a job in the field of medical billing and coding because you needed hand on experience to get the job in the record and the school program

School program of medical billing and coding was a new program for Sanford Brown Institute which didn't have an extern program so I could get credit hours they had a career service program who sent out on temporary job sites in Bethesda but they didn't plan out either. So I walked out of my student loan owning the government $12,000,00 when the loan was only for $8000.00 with no job yes when you finished school the work study job ended as well we was stuck with bills to pay no job. It hurt the marriage I had to change fields found an agency a job who was looking for substitute teachers followed all the rules passed all the test CPR, First Aid, Drug test, background check did a test for CPS cleared that test as well because a substitute teachers for 3 years made the money to hold it down that how we got into our rented house where as soon as well moved in we had admitted borders everybody wanted to moved in our layed back nice home me and my husband had to have the good sense to say NO. The ones that did move in stuck's with $1000.00 gas bill I paid water bill and my husband held down the electric people and their children was trying to lay around my house cigarette smokes, everybody with the habits had to be told they couldn't move in and I couldn't understand why people

Why people over they age of 18 yrs. old want to live with me and my husband Rodney destroying our peace our love our happiness because of demonic spirits jealousy, wicked people drug addicts, jailbirds, murders, liars and thieves all kinds of people thought that our house rented was the party house. We celebrated birthdays parties to our kids and grandkids we did cook outs for us because my husband Rodney like friends over I almost watched a female get killed in my house. Street lady walkers was almost invited to my house I don't play that, I had to put a stop to it all. We had water damage in the basement our upper bedrooms all looked like trash, all dirty because people who was there never learned how to clean-up, food was in my dish washer being used as a washing machine, people bought bad bugs in my house because they was so naive they were getting mattress off the street I was going through a pretty bad transition when (our) my mother was ill, it caused alot of problems in my marriage with all the jealous people that surrounded us with their demonic spirits. Lot of things went on in our house. We did enjoy living there but my husband Rodney wasn't making the money to hold it down.

That my husband put the gas bill in his name but it still was an issue electrictly got off we had to live by candle flashlights fireplace which was nice I was working he was working but not managing his money correct people was begging for money every week, he got paid. We had it real hard it was winter

I was ill & cold getting sick had to stay in the cold so my daughter knew I was ill so she and I decided together that me and my husband would come stay with her because we could no longer afford a $1,500.00 rent bought down to $1200.00 a month with a leaky basement with utility bills & car insurance food & toiletry threw it was to much to leave in the nice looking house me and my husband needed a cheaper place just for us to live no grown up living in our house or place which ever now I am disabled permanently he is working making good money but because of everything we went through we have grown apart we loved each other never cheated on each other but we have our own lives we are living we share our grandkids. From time to time never strayed sexual but by we are not together we final did have a honeymoon but that was interrupted as well after 9 yrs. it was our 1st honeymoon Econolog Inn we went to the new restaurant South Beach $100 for dinner upper scale restaurant after that we wanted to stay in a nice hotel we look and looked and looked but we couldn't find anything every hotel we went to was booked solid on May 19, 20015 ain't that something we was getting despaired because he had to get up early because he was working in VA & had to leave @ 4:00 am so the only thing available that night was Econo Lodge $100.00 a night we took it. He was tired and so was I. I wanted to do his feet give him a pedicure so we could make love and go to sleep why are I finished the pedicure we get a call from his cousin wanting to talk when it was there for us to make love we just never ever been uninterrupted by somebody family not family whoever, alone intimacy is something me and my husband have never had and she got her teeth pull who figure she would want to talk we told her take her meds she was talking about her mouth was hurt do you see why smoking cigarettes and talk what do you expect. So that cause a big argument because I put the truth on social media she didn't speak to me for months, did she think that I cared she interrupt my sex with my husband @ that point I didn't care of it was your cousin he that night was all mines especial since we never been alone since

Never been alone with this man since we got married never had a honeymoon. Never was alone with this man. We worked right after we got married and for ten years we were never alone ever we got married. We went on marriage retreat his mother was calling when is it over and it was amazing he was so tentative to me I thought it was hope but it didn't last it's all good I have another chance in love and God will see us through I am not putting down my husband but soon to be ex but when something is not meant to be because of the timing is wrong no matter what you do it won't work certain things works very well and our intimacy was always amazing but the timing was always off. Thanks be to God for his glory I plead the blood of Jesus going forth. Since we been married always been somebody around trying to get his attention that belong to me from him. And personal I was tired of it all. Everybody having something to say in reference to our marriage people not wanting us to get married people not coming to the wedding to ppl trying to analyze our marriage the jealousy the hatred he had to tell me his cousin wasn't an interruption when he knew we was making love for me in my mind it was the last straw, but I realize she did it on purpose because she had no man so that feel under jealousy: Who calls a person after you post it on the (facebook) no interruption on social media she talking about she thought that it didn't apply to her your must be crazy husband and wife time is called honeymoon. Get a man get a husband you will see. Some people think they above everything but when it comes to me and my man you are just like the rest last, I talk 10:30 pm. we wasn't living together for this honeymoon it was our last chance at love, with each other the nine-year wedding anniversary for us, so we wanted to be alone, attitudes flared drama queen was active. PPl always thought they had a right to come between me & my husband, when we got married after the I do's he had the phone up to his ear taken a phone call, we had no honeymoon.

And when we tried to have one cousin called to talk so 9 yrs emotional roller coaster for us, but it is so sad because this marriage is true love, we been in love since he was 17 yrs. old and I was 19 yrs. old when we first met I was working in a restaurant cooking carry out food we saw each other across a crowded room a grill hot grease & lots of customer we met eyes to eyes. He order a submarine fila fish sub with mayo & onions a whole sub he play the jute box & Sears and Roboacks I came up to the counter we talked a lot I put his sub together with wedge fries he paid me & I gave to him we stared in each others eyes he played a couple more songs and left he did it a couple times before I saw him get arrested off of his motorcycle, we talked a couple more time I wanted him he wanted me we were in love. He came to my neighborhood we went downstairs to a neighbor house made sweet love to each other and I never saw him the same again we both felt guilty because we were not cheaters his girlfriend he caught cheating on him my boyfriend was always going out of town so I figured he cheated on me but 20 yrs later found out he didn't but my third husband had came back to me after he broke up with the cheating girlfriend and she not his girlfriend and he don't like her. But I immediately told him that you need to marry her because she's the mother of your child. My 1st husband got me pregnant my mother had a talk with him and worst thing I knew they didn't even ask me. We was getting married my 1st husband and mother decided for me so, I found out he took some jewelry from his mother or whatever so she put him out and his now ex wife gave birth to his son and place him in his arm, he was sorting his wild oats while she was pregnant, because one was his ex-girlfriend but he married this chic, because the mother was ashamed to be in church woman and have a grandchild illegitimate a bastor child, so they got married he wanted a baby girl, so now at that point they were in agreement a girl came to that marriage 2 yrs later but it still did not last, 10 yrs later he was a stranged from that marriage, because it had no love in the divorce by phone 25 yrs late he came back where I lived where he was really from, we were on another job I was on doing inventory for over a year we met @ a Glass Robaes Co our eyes met yet again, and we worked for two different branch office ME CAMP SPRING HIM SILVER SPRING, but end up@ same location he was walking around instead of working asking people have they seen the girl with the orange burned hair that was me. I was on thee other hand was working, at the end of the day. Always help my boss clean up do the tags and put them in place neatly. And we saw each other again he waited until I was finished to walk me to my car, my daughter's car mines had just gotten reposed.

2 mos before I lost my 626 Madza 2000, because it cost to much 24 percent interest, I was set up 525 a month car note, you would think I had a Mecedez. That's what my loan I was set up for failure and failed it miserably.

My husband Rodney gave me a car and sold it. Gave the one my mom gave back to the estate but God has bless me getting ready get a new used one as we speak, praise the Lord, God is great. And nobody but nobody can take this one away from me. I had one be free before this one (4) two years and it was old 1997 Chevy Lumina Green grass green I pay $1300.00 4 door put $3000 into this car no thank you not again. It hurt me to sale my car but the engine was going bad, I had to be towed home from church. Now that is sad, August 2005 got sold after hubby looked at it a couple of times he said sale it.

I am learning more and more and more about me. I have learned (Pisces)—woman like myself for example is exuberant and cheerful, outgoing, and affectionate. I am a dreamer attentive lover. I desire respect I have a good sense of humor, I appreciate kindness and I return it. Peace lover, magnanimous. Sexy personality, good at keeping secrets, sympathic, trustworthy (Aries)—man the ram I am very much attracted to Aries the ram my sign is in Neptune and an Aries man is in Mars. Amiable diplomatic always ready to help others. Adentorous. Great sense of human. Loves to enjoy life, totally active and restless. More emotional than practical. A good motivator spiritually and God fearing. Good looking and sexy. Faithful lover, hasty decision maker and brainy and clever. My ex-husband Rodney of 10 yrs. Marriage. We basically are so busy we barely have time to share our love for one another but when we come to get it like firecrackers going off he's the fire and I am the water that puts the fire out we are very much attracted to each other, but how do you make it last with all the interference in our lives and all the jealousy ppl who don't want to see us together how does it work forever because forever is along time.

God never said the weapons wouldn't form he said they wouldn't prosper, because no weapons formed against me or you shall prosper that is what God said. Deliver me and you from every evil. And while you at it . . . Put on the full armor of God which is another form of protection father God constantly rebuking Satan in the name of Jesus sealed by the blood for your protection you don't have God you don't have nothing he shows me over and over and over etc . . . . How powerful he is and we can do all things through Christ which strengthens us. But without God our lives will never be changed because he works for our good living off of his strengths, yes, Lord, I believe if it hadn't been for the Lord. I wouldn't be living today to speak on this. And in advance father God I thank you for the love agapey to everyone. This week God is going to do exceedly abundantly above all things, we ask because we serve an on time God halleljuh it is written it is done. Heavenly father when I am tired you give me strength to go on when discouraged you give me hope. When I am afraid you are my peace for all of this father God I thank you, having your treasures in heaven is a wonderful thing learn to collect moments not things. I am a woman of God in this way in the same way, let your light shine before others, that they may see your good deed and glorify your father in heaven for making it all possible he works for your good without him it's impossible to see the glory in it. Every day is not going to be a bed of roses but when your challenges come know that God is with you and through prayers he makes your journey easier to go through because he is there carrying all the steps of the way. Even when we can't see it he is working for your good. Be a good stewards be patient Jesus answered "I am the way and the truth and the light no one comes to the father accept through me believing salvation, praise him.

Blessed is the person who knows Jesus as their Savor. Heavenly father I declare that I can do all things through Christ who gives me strength. I speak to the mountains in my life and say "Be moved"! I declare blessings, favor, and victory over my present and my future life. When people want to know about your personal life they should come directly to you instead of everybody else gossiping. The 1st thing you should do when you wake up is tell God thanks because it could have went the other way. Never be ashamed of what you went through God will use your story for his glory. I am thankful to be bless for the privilege to be able to be a blessing to others lives, and be able to show God unconditional love agapey the joy God gives us in our hearts is overflowing indescribable thank you Jesus, just when Satan tries to put you down Jesus lifts you up and over. When any obstacles in your way I am thankful for God is amazing provision just when you don't know how you are going to pay a bill or put food on your table, I pray to God and immediately he comes through and provides money exactly to the very penny, what you need to overcome these obstacles and I am thankful we serve and awesome amazing God Roman 1:16 the righteous shall live by faith: For I am not ashamed of the gospel for it is power of God for salvation to everyone who believes to the Jesus and also to the Greek, for its the righteous of God is revealed from faith for faith as it is written the righteous shall live by faith. God wrath on unrighteous for the wrath of God is revealed from heaven against all ungodliness and unrighteousness of men what can be known about God is plain to them. Invisible attributes, namely his eternal power since the creation of the world in the things that have been made so they are without excuse for although they knew God. They did not honor him as God or give thanks to him, but they became futile in their thinking and their foolish hearts were darkened claiming to be wise they became fools and exchanged there glory of the immortal God for image resembling mortal man and birds and animals creeping things therefore God gave them up in the lusts of their hearts to impurity to the dishonoring of their bodies amongst.

because they exchanged the truths about God for a lie and worshipped and served the creatures rather than the creator, who is blessed forever, Amen. For this reason God gave them up to dishonorable passions, for their their women exchanged natural relations for those that contrary to nature and the men likewise gave up natural relations with women and were consumed with passion for one another, men comitting shameless acts with, an and since they did not see fit to acknowledge God, God gave them up to a debated mind to do what ought not be done, they are filled with all manner of unrighteousness, evil, covetousness malice. They are full of envy, murder, strife, deceit, maliciousness. They are gossiping, slanders, haters of God, insolent, naughty, boastful, inventor of evil disobedient to parents foolish, faithless, heartless, ruthless. God's righteous judgment everyone who judges, for in passing judgment on another you condemn yourself because you the judge, practice the very same things, we know that the judgment or God rightly falls on those who practice such things. And yet do them yourself, that you will not escape judgment of God or do you presume on the riches of his kindness and forbearance and patience, not knowing that God's kindness is meant to lead you to repentance but because of your hard and impatient heart you are stoned up with wrath for yourself on the day of wrath when God's righteous judgment will be revealed He will render to each one according to his works, to those who by patience in well doing seek for glory and honor and immortality, he will give eternal life but for those who are self-seeking and do not obey the truth, but obey unrighteousness there will be wrath and fury there will be tribulation and distress for every human being who does evil the Jew first and also the Greek. but glory and honor and peace for everyone who does good, the Jew first and the Greek for God shows no partiality. And alot of things have come to past which I will start with my daughter Dominique she was pregnant at 1 month lets say 2 yrs ago but she was saying to me that she not feeling good so I came over her aptment and she was walking down the street to the car she was wabbing funny from side to side saying she was in a lot of pain I knew she was pregnant but God came to me immediately and said get your family in the car & take this child/adult of your to the hospital why as soon as I got everybody and got to the hospital she had to have emergency surgery the baby was in her tubes and the doctor informed me that if I had not gotten her to the hospital when I did the baby which was growing in her tubes would have burst and the both would have died so if it had had not been for the glory of God through my understanding of God listening to God and doing his will my daughter would have died my family has been through a lot of tremoil since then but because of no faith and trust in God alot of bicknering has been going on few years. But God said it shall come to an end and that's why alot of thing has happen that has not been good for any of us. But I put all my faith and trust in God because he works for your good my God is a healer, deliverer savior of our salvation my sister tried all she could to not only deceive others but all of us as well she tried to get away with all of my mother thousands of dollar and leave us with change but thanks to the smarts of my sister Tonya and my daughter Dominique and myself we stopped her from ending up with the majority of our deceased mothers money she did get a way with all funeral arrangements being made by her and controlling the last hospice stay of our mothers life but when it came down to it even though our mother didn't want her to receive anything from her she received the smallest amount of money from her estate and I owe this all to God because if it had not been him and with her with no will

In place legally the 4th daughter was through the courts about to rob all 3 other siblings with her lies and deceit but God is a healer he saw it all the knew the devil in her was not going to win that's what she was doing was totally wrong she got the life insurance policy money of $20,000.00 or $2500,00 of the estate we receive the most of the estate, because God work for your good and so I advice everyone get a legal will, protect your family the loving family you may have when people are alive won't be the same loving people in your family when death occurs people changes for different reason demonic spirits show up and all you can say is who are three demonic people they wasn't that way when your matriarch who controls the love balance the provision of your family the balance the respect died after she died. The patriarch who controls the family the balance of respect, when the love ones die and the feeling of not enough godliness is in place before each of these gospel godly loving leaders leave go home to paradise to join God above, turn on each other change for the worst protect your family I put a hedge of protect on my entire family my son & daughter, all my grandkids, my husband, myself my Christian family. Protect all my nieces and nephews extended nieces and nephews all my cousin in laws. Before disaster strikes your family and move on and have a life.

Yes, and they both can heal and grow & love each other through it you can't change the past of the Hurt done from the elder sibling ....but you can have a loving trusting & more secure friendship beyond the hurt, damage & pain.... and starting with forgiven sincerely in our hearts and both can grow from it, with Godly love agapey love from God..... I too enjoyed what i have grown from God about empathy, not narcissistic personality, it the most hurtful you can suffer from family.... without God in the hearts.... She lost the most, but we both lost.... because our children and grand children are suffering distance not to mention social distancing not from covid-19, but from hatred because we the only two siblings with children.... the loving friendship & lack of loving relationships that wasn't there, that she & i needed so badly desired, from me, as a mature talented mom figure.... as well so they both took a lost and growth is what was needed from both. Through forgiveness. Forgiveness aint for the other person forgiveness is for you, & me to cater to our family's so they can come back together in a loving relationship.

.for God to bless you & me .....Which we both can learn through forgiveness, open doors for us both and hearts can heal...let go let God..... not only being true to self but saying sorry □ with a sincere honey heart....it can mend broken fences. Snd heal our families.... the end in add on...

Because so much was taken away when the children and grand child suffered the most.... God is love and that what he wants from us to learn to love one another agapey Love comes from God.

THANK 🙏 YOU LORD FOR loving me even when I am sick 😁 🙏 😃 🖤 ♥

with sinus infection 🙏 😔 & have a cold ☐ and needing time & space

to myself... loving others from a far touching base, checking in, checking on

others ... a Germopho from the heart ♥. Loving everyone... I told a story once

of my accident at birth ♥ my mom went for a baby check up at DC General

hospital ✚ when it was in business now closed..... and the elevator drop 6 floor

below I have a vessel in my head being watched by the doctors even til today..... I

am a miracle child /adult grown Queen.... 😊 with love in her heart.... of Gold....

I pray that everyone has a happy healthy Christmas 🎄 🙏 ♥ that God gives you

🙏 😃 through prayers..... pray without ceasing the desires of your heart......if not

comes close to it..... Love you all.....Mature sophisticated lady, that wants the

best for everyone God blessed me with two wonderful babies one that challenges

me, and 1 that loves unconditionally.... love them both the same & 4 beautiful

talented grandkids and I blended son ♥ Jonte' full grown.... thank you lord for

the blessings.... i love them all & all of my church ⛪ Family blended family

one of my church daugta Meka Amõr & the G3 grands, love them all growing

beautifully around the holiday has always been sad for me my grandma 😊 Ruth

whom has to raise me bcos my mom was ill from the hospital ✚ drop, stayed in the hospital 4mos... I stay 2mos. The day after Thanksgiving was her birthday, she gone and very much missed. But for Christmas 🎄 my mom always wanted to be Mrs Claus 🎅 to family she was she gave gift 🎁's to all her blended grandkids / great grandkids....I miss her some much she went home to heaven as well....but I am emotional around the holidays..... I have a special man in my life that loves 💘 💓 ❤ me through it all 1yr going two month Jae, he is incredible with me.... but I am thinking of the elders right now grandpa my Daddy whom is also in heaven.... so if I seem a lil distracted or distant it's because I am miss my elders. My ❤ is pure no offense, to anyone.... me & my mom was like besties..... I love everyone thank You God for the wonderful many blessings You bestow upon me..... And choosing me to be your own name written in the book of lambs..... ever hair on my head is counted by God so is yours....but I am talking about me now......enjoy this holiday wear your masks social distancing, the ABC song ♪ wash them hands ✋🧼 stay home, if possible, take God on your travels, be loving & don't try to mess up no one holiday not even your own...do what ever you have to do to stay healthy....

God bless you all & peace ✌ ❤ ☺ be with you humbling myself have peace that surpassesallunderstanding... be curious to others ...... the end!!! The Author Angeli Lowery. Whom is now a grubhub driver part time getting it done.

My bad have peace that surpasses all understanding respect one another space do whatever you have to do to stay safe 🎧💯 covid-19 free God bless you all God/ Messiah Jehovah, Jaire Jehovah Nissy, our soul provider pray to Him he has our back. to get to God we have to go through Jesus Jesus didn't come in to the world to condemn the world but so the world might be saved for all whom has faith and believe in Him that the way to heaven. God chose us. By loving us 1st. Believe that.

Printed in the United States
By Bookmasters